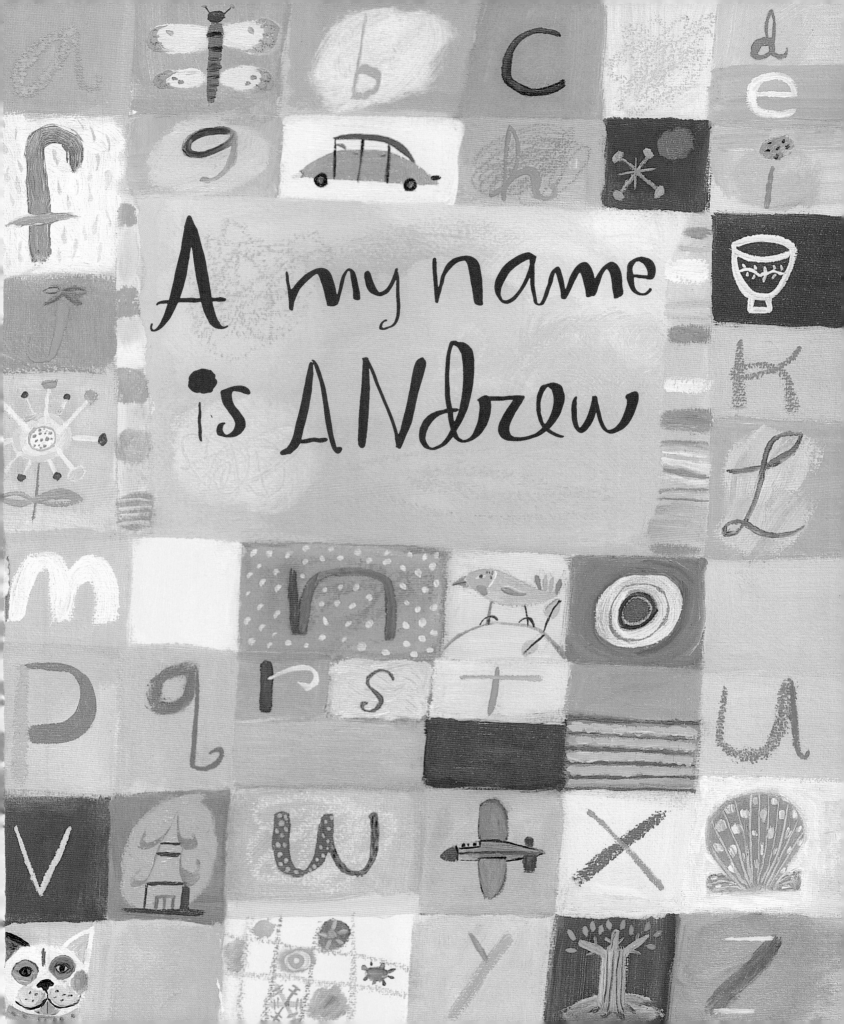

For my grandchildren...in alphabetical order

Bridget Ashley, Erin Nan, Mary Claire,

Matthew Robert, Megan Elizabeth and Sean Patrick

–Mary McManus Burke

Text copyright ©2003 by Mary McManus Burke
Illustrations copyright ©2003 by Donna Ingemanson

All About Kids Publishing
6280 San Ignacio Ave., Ste. D
San Jose, CA 95119

Editor: Lisa M. Tooker
Book Design: Libby Ellis

Manufactured in China

Library of Congress Cataloging-in-Publication Data

Burke, Mary McManus.
A, my name is Andrew / by Mary McManus Burke ; illustrated by Donna
Ingemanson.
p. cm.
Summary: From all over the United States, each of twenty-six children
describes their activities in a paragraph featuring the letter of the
alphabet that matches their first name and the city in which they live.
ISBN 0-9710278-5-4 (hardcover)
1. English language--Alphabet--Juvenile literature. 2. City and town
life--United States--Juvenile literature. [1. Alphabet. 2. City and town
life.] I. Ingemanson, Donna, ill. II. Title.
PE1155 .B86 2002
428.1--dc21
[[
2001007456

A my name is ANdrew

Written by Mary McManus Burke

Illustrated by Donna Ingemanson

all about kids
publishing

SAN JOSE

 **My name is Andrew** & I come from Augusta. On an **autumn** afternoon my Aunt Adrienne **always** takes me on our annual **apple** picking adventure. After driving awhile,

We arrive at an ancient abbey where there are acres and acres of apple trees. Our arms are full as we unload my aunt's automobile. We always share our abundance of apples with all our neighbors in the adjacent apartments.

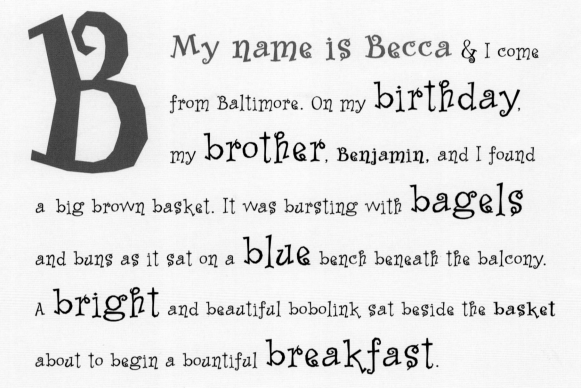

My name is Becca & I come from Baltimore. On my birthday, my brother, Benjamin, and I found a big brown basket. It was bursting with bagels and buns as it sat on a blue bench beneath the balcony. A bright and beautiful bobolink sat beside the basket about to begin a bountiful breakfast.

cuckoo! cuckoo!

C My name is Claire & I come from Connecticut. In our cozy, carpeted country cottage I have a collection of clamorous colorful cuckoo clocks. They completely cover the cherry credenza and cause countless loud cries of complaint from my cute cousins.

D

My name is Derrick & I come from **Detroit**. One dark and dreary day in December my **Dad decided** we'd do something different for dinner. Dad **drove** us directly downtown to the Dinosaur **Diner**.

DINER

OPEN

We had a **delicious** dinner and a deep discussion on dachshunds and **desserts**, **diving** and duty. It was definitely different!

E My name is Enrica & I live in El Paso. I **enjoy** encouraging my enthusiastic elephant, Esperanza, to **engage** in energetic, exhilarating exercise early each morning at **eight**.

Esperanza has an endless amount of endurance. She's an eyeful in her **elaborately** and exquisitely embroidered exercise outfits, and her engraved enameled **earrings**.

F

My name is Fai & I live in Fresno. My four faithful **friends** and I go **fishing** for flounder each Friday afternoon from four to **five**. We look **fabulous** in our five fuzzy feathered fedoras. It's fantastic **fun!**

G

My name is Gabrielle & I live in Greensboro. My **grandparents** go to the **greatest** garage sales in the galaxy. They've given me a grand guitar, green **gloves**, a glistening goblet, a **globe**, great games, goldfish and a graceful giraffe. Go Grandma and Grandpa, **GO!**

golf club

gyroscope

My name is Halia & I live in Honolulu. My half-brother Havika and I have the happiest, hula-loving **hamsters** in the **hemisphere**. However, they have a habit of hiding in hampers, handbags, hatboxes and **hedges**. Honestly, when that happens, we need help to find them and bring them home in a **hurry** before they get **homesick**. They need heartfelt hugs every hour.

INCREDIBLE!

I

My name is Isaiah & I live in Indianapolis. With my incredible imagination, I can be inside an igloo in an instant, ice-skating indoors, visiting the city of Independence, or climbing an immense ice cream iceberg inch by delicious inch. If it's an interesting adventure, I can imagine it!

igloo

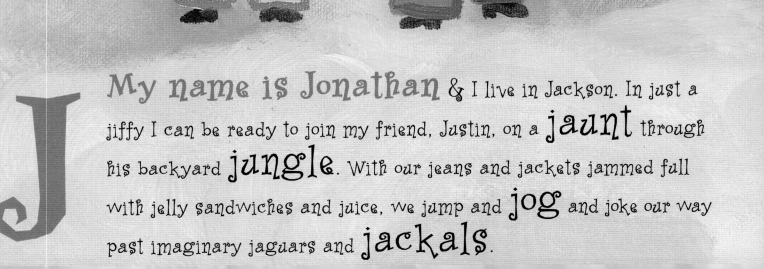

J My name is Jonathan & I live in Jackson. In just a jiffy I can be ready to join my friend, Justin, on a **jaunt** through his backyard **jungle**. With our jeans and jackets jammed full with jelly sandwiches and juice, we jump and **jog** and joke our way past imaginary jaguars and **jackals**.

K

My name is Kayla & I live in Kansas City. My cousin and I keep my kitten, Kyle clothed in khaki knickers and a colorful knitted kerchief. His knapsack contains kiwis and kumquats from the kitchen cupboard. The day Kyle followed us to kindergarten he just knew he was "King of the Class" when the kids kept kissing his kind and cute little face.

kyle

backpack

Kiwis

kumquats

L

Long Island

My name is Leonardo & I live in Long Island. Following a lunch of lasagna and **lemonade**, I like to visit our **large**, local library. The library always looks lovely with its landscaped **lilacs** and lilies.

lemonade

Lasagna

Liliana, the **librarian**, loans me a long list of books on ladybugs, lobsters, lakes and **lighthouses.**

library

lilacs

lilies

I **love** to read, and I've learned lots of different lessons, while reading at my leisure.

Lakes

M

My name is Margarita &
I live in Miami.

One misty Monday morning during the month of May, Mama made a
mountain of marvelous mango muffins for Miguel and me. Mr. Mendoza,
our mild-mannered mailman, managed to arrive at mid-morning
just in time for Mama's memorable munchies.

N

My name is Niara & I live in New York. Since November we have had nice next-door neighbors with a **newborn** baby named Navarro. **Normally** his parents give Navarro nine **nighttime** feedings to nourish him. We watched Navarro being fed in his newly decorated nautical **nursery**.

My name is Oki & I live in Oakland. Our one and only pet, an opossum named Orino, wears outrageous, ornate **overalls** and plays the **oboe**. He eats only onions, okra and olives. In my opinion, that's okay occasionally, but **oranges** would give Orino a sweeter option.

P

Perfect!

My name is Paloma & I live in Pueblo. I **prefer** to practice the **piano** and play the piccolo in the pink parlor, while wearing my **purple** pants and plaid pullover. I make sure my posture is perfect during my piano performances. I also put my hair in **pigtails** and pick musical pieces to **play** that positively will please my parents and make them **proud** of me.

Q

My name is Quinlan & I live in Quincy. I'm the only **quintuplet** in my town. My brothers and sisters and I have acquired a quintet of **quality** quaint **quilts**, five quarts of quartz and five quiet quail. Any questions?

R

My name is Robert & I live in Rochester. My reliable friend, Ryan and I have reading races regularly. **Right** now, it's

a tie. We **remember** and revere the remarkable rewards and ribbons we've received for reading reams and reams of books about **reptiles**, ranches, raccoons and railroads. **Reading** is our recreation and it gives us time to relax.

S

My name is Son & I live in San Jose. In the summertime my sister and I spend every single second we can at the **seashore**. We swim and search the sand for seashells. We **savor** our supper of spring rolls and spicy shrimp as we sit on the shoreline and watch the spectacular **sunset**.

T

My name is Teresa & I live in Tuscaloosa. My two true-hearted friends and I have tea every Tuesday from **ten** to two. We sit at the teak table on the triangular terrace and talk 'til three-thirty. We are **truly** thankful and treasure this time **together**.

U

My name is Umberto & I live in Urbandale. My uncles and I are undeniably united in our unending amazement at the **unique** appeal of the **unicycle**. Unfortunately, we don't understand why we are unable to ride it uphill after umpteen **unforgettable** undertakings. It's utterly unbelievable.

 **My name is Vanessa** & I live in Virginia. My family often visits and vacations in a verdant **valley** surrounded by vintage **Victorian** villages. The valley is lush with vineyards, and the gardens within the valley grow a huge **variety** of **vegetables**. The vegetables contain very valuable vitamins. We load the voluminous **van** with overflowing vegetables and off we go! The view from atop our vehicle is beyond my **vocabulary**.

W

My name is William & I live in Whitefish. We wake up in winter to the whitest **wonderland** in the whole wide **world**. Whatever we wear is woven and woolen so that when we walk in the **woods** our wardrobe stays warm and **windproof**.

whitefish

X

My name is Xavier & I live in Xenia. Each Xmas season the sound of the **xylophone** is heard across the land.

Y

My name is Yoluta & I live in Yuma. Yesterday I fed yummy yogurt and yellow yams to my young **yak** in our yard.

Z

My name is Zachary &
I live in Zanesville.

We have zesty, zippy zebras that play the
zither and love zucchini. They're really zany
and love to sing as they zigzag through
the zoo.

Glossary

autumn The season between summer and winter

annual Something that happens every year.

adventure An unusual experience.

ancient Very, very old.

abbey A church.

acre A large piece of land that is 4,840 square yards.

abundance Plenty of something; more than enough.

adjacent Next to or nearby.

apartment One room or several rooms to live in.

bobolink An American migratory songbird.

bountiful Plenty; lots and lots of something.

Charlottesville A city in the commonwealth of Virginia.

cherry A deep red color.

clamorous Noisy, very loud.

complaint Not happy with a situation.

countless Too many to be counted.

credenza A cabinet with no legs; a piece of furniture.

cuckoo clock A clock with a mechanical bird that makes a loud noise.

dachshund A small dog with a long body, short legs and drooping ears.

derrick A machine for lifting and moving heavy objects.

Detroit The largest city in the state of Michigan.

digger A tool, part of a machine for digging.

discussion To talk about.

duty Something someone must do or ought to show.

elaborately Very fancy; detailed.

El Paso The fourth largest city in the state of Texas.

embroidered Decorated with needlework designs on cloth.

enameled Painted with a shiny hard surface.

encouraging Feeling of confidence, support.

energetic Peppy; active.

engraved A carved design.

enthusiastic Very eager to do something.

exhilarating Lively, to "perk up."

exquisitely Beautiful.

eyeful Something nice to see.

fabulous Fantastic, wonderful, great.

faithful Loyal and trustworthy.

fedora A type of hat.

flounder A fish.

Fresno A city in the state of California.

galaxy A large group of stars and planets.

glistening To shine softly.

goblet A drinking glass with a stem and a base.

Greensboro A city in the state of North Carolina.

hamper A large covered container sometimes used for laundry.

hedges A fence of shrubs or low growing trees.

hemisphere One half of a sphere, especially of the earth.

Honolulu The capital and the largest city in Hawaii.

hula-loving Loves dancing the hula.

igloo An Eskimo house, usually dome-shaped and built of blocks of snow.

immense Very large, huge.

incredible Hard to believe.

Independence The fourth largest city in the state of Missouri.

Indianapolis The largest city in the state of Indiana.

Jackson A city in the state of Tennessee.

jackals Dog-like animals found in Asia and Africa.

jaguars Large cat-like animals with black spots.

jaunt A short trip.

jiffy An instant, a moment.

Kansas City The largest city in the state of Missouri.

kiwis A brown, hairy, egg-sized fruit grown primarily in New Zealand.

khaki A yellow-brown color or cloth.

knapsack A bag worn on the back.

kumquats An orange-colored fruit about the size of a small plum.

landscaped An area of land improved with planting.

Long Island An island that is part of the state of New York.

lush A rich growth of vegetation.

mango A sweet, juicy fruit.

memorable Something remarkable, worth remembering.

Miami The second largest city in the state of Florida.

misty A light fog; drizzle.

nautical Having to do with ships, sailors or navigation.

New York A city in the state of New York.

nourish To feed.

Oakland A city in the state of California.

oboe A musical instrument.

okra A vegetable.

opossum A nocturnal (active at night) mammal.

ornate Lots of fancy decorations.

outrageous Shocking or offensive.

parlor A formal living room.

piccolo A small musical instrument of the flute family.

pigtails Long braids of hair.

Pueblo A city in the state of Colorado.

quail Small game birds, like partridges.

quartz A brilliant crystal stone.

Quincy A city in the commonwealth of Massachusetts.

quintet Five of something.

quintuplet One of five babies born at the same time.

reliable Someone you can depend on and trust.

remarkable Extraordinary.

revere To feel deep respect and love for.

Rochester A city in the state of Minnesota.

San Jose The third largest city in the state of California.

savor To taste with enjoyment.

shoreline The land along the edge of an ocean, a river or a lake.

spicy shrimp Stir-fried shrimp cooked in salt, pepper and spices.

teak Yellowish-brown wood.

tender Gentle, careful, sensitive to others' feelings.

treasure Appreciate, value or love.

Tuscaloosa A city in the state of Alabama.

unbelievable Difficult to believe; incredible.

unicycle A riding device with one wheel and pedals, but no handlebars.

umpteen A great number of, very many.

Urbandale A city in the state of Iowa.

verdant Green, grassy, covered with green vegetation.

vineyards Land where grapevines grow.

vintage Excellent; old-time.

vocabulary All of the words used and understood by a person.

wardrobe A collection of clothes usually belonging to one person

Whitefish A town in the state of Montana.

woolen Yarn spun from the fibers of sheep hair.

woven To make a fabric by interlacing threads or yarn.

Xenia A city in the state of Ohio.

Xmas Christmas.

xylophone A musical instrument.

yams Sweet potatoes.

yak A stocky, long-haired animal.

Yuma A city in the state of Arizona.

Zanesville A city in the state of Ohio.

zany Silly, funny.

zesty Lively, excited.

zippy Full of energy.

zither A musical instrument.